Beginning Phonics
WORKBOOK

Scholastic Inc.

Dear Parent,

Help your child learn to read with phonics! Phonics is the relationship between the sounds of *spoken* language and the letters that represent those sounds in *written* language. Research shows that kids who master phonics become confident readers.

Bob Books: Beginning Phonics Workbook makes learning phonics fun! Kids will practice making the connection between sounds and letters and begin to **read simple words**. Activities include matching, rhyming, word mazes, writing letters and words, and of course, reading stories!

This workbook is perfect for kids who know their letters and are **just beginning to learn to read**. It can be completed alongside the Bob Books Stage 1 decodable books or on its own.

Because the sounds and letters are introduced in a systematic way, you and your child should **move through the activities in order**. For each activity, read the instructions to your child. Then help them get started and be available to answer questions. When your child completes the workbook, make sure to hang up the **achievement certificate** so they can show off their hard work!

We wish you and your child many happy hours practicing phonics with Mat, Sam, Dot, Mac, and all the other Bob Books friends!

— The Bob Books team

Copyright © 2025 Bob Books Publications, LLC. All rights reserved. Published by Scholastic Inc., *Publishers since 1920.* Published by arrangement with Bob Books® Publications, LLC. SCHOLASTIC and associated logos are trademarks and/or registered trademarks of Scholastic Inc. Bob Books and the Bob Books logo are trademarks or registered trademarks of Bob Books Publications, LLC.

The publisher does not have any control over and does not assume any responsibility for author or third-party websites or their content.

No part of this publication may be reproduced, stored in a retrieval system, or transmitted in any form or by any means, electronic, mechanical, photocopying, recording, or otherwise, or used to train any artificial intelligence technologies, without written permission of the publisher. For information regarding permission, write to Scholastic Inc., Attention: Permissions Department, 557 Broadway, New York, NY 10012.

ISBN 978-1-5461-6977-2   10 9 8 7 6 5 4 3 2   25 26 27 28 29
Printed in the U.S.A. 40   First printing, 2025
Read aloud icon © Getty Images   Cover art by Amy Jindra and Karen Wall
Cover design by Rainbow Educational Concepts   Book design by Rainbow Educational Concepts

Table of Contents

Welcome to the World of Bob Books!	4–5
Letters *Aa*, *Mm*, *Tt*, *Ss*	6–9
Story Time!	10
Letters *Cc*, *Dd*	11–14
Story Time!	15
Letters *Oo*, *Hh*, *Rr*, *Gg*	16–23
Story Time!	24
Letter *Bb*	25–33
Story Time!	34
Letters *Ii*, *Nn*	35–43
Story Time!	44
Letters *Pp*, *Jj*, *Ww*	45–53
Story Time!	54
Letters *Uu*, *Ff*	55–63
Story Time!	64
Letters *Ee*, *Kk*	65–73
Story Time!	74
Letters *Ll*, *Xx*	75–82
Story Time!	83
Letters *Vv*, *Yy*, *Zz*, *Qq*	84–92
Story Time!	93
"I Read the Whole Book!"® Certificate	95

Welcome to the world of Bob Books!

Color the Bob Books friends below.
Then draw a picture of yourself!

Letter Aa

Say the picture name.
Listen to the beginning sound.
What sound do you hear?

The word **apple** begins with the **short a sound, /a/**.*

Trace the letters.

Color each uppercase *A* red.
Color each lowercase *a* blue.

*Letters between slash marks represent the sound a letter makes. For example, /m/ represents "mmm".

Letter Mm

Say the picture name.
Listen to the beginning sound.
What sound do you hear?

The word **moon** begins with the m sound, /m/.

Trace the letters.

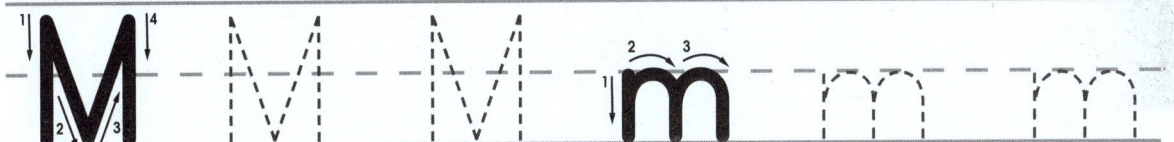

Mat's name begins with /m/.
He is glad to meet you!

What's your name?

Write it below.

_____

Letter Tt

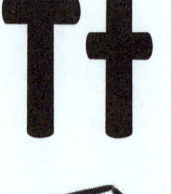

Say the picture name.
Listen to the beginning sound.
What sound do you hear?

The word **table** begins with the
t sound, /t/.

Trace the letters.

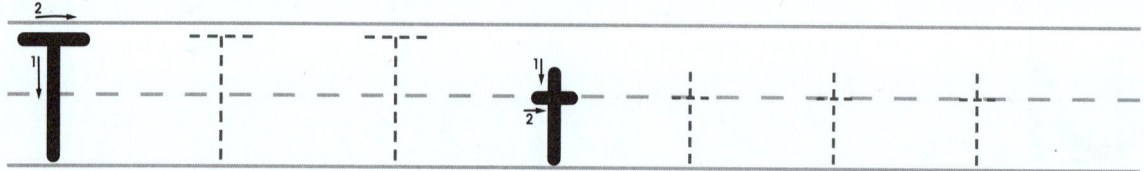

Say each picture name. If it begins with /t/, draw a line to *Tt*.

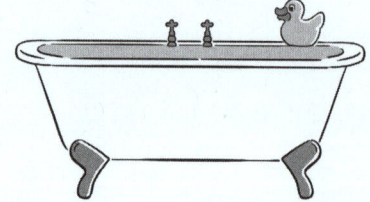

Letter Ss

Say the picture name.
Listen to the beginning sound.
What sound do you hear?

The word **sun** begins with the
s sound, /s/.

Trace the letters.

Color each uppercase *S* red.
Color each lowercase *s* blue.

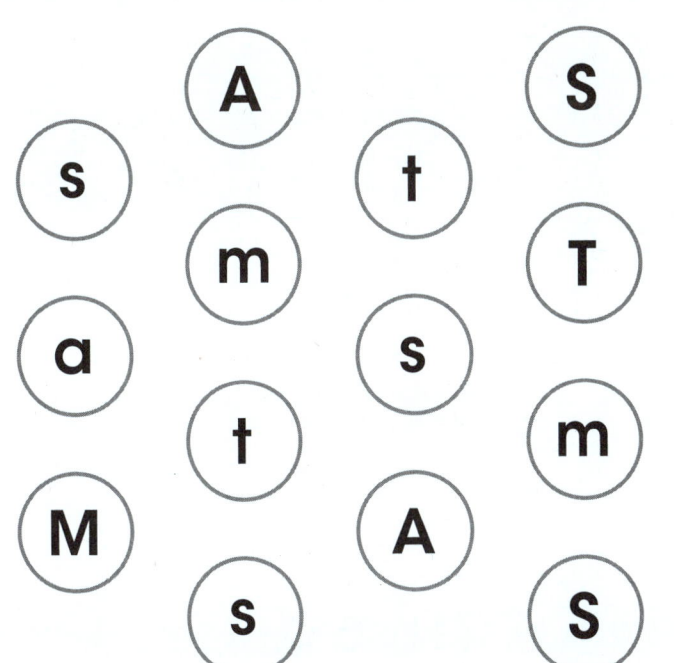

9

Story Time!

Trace the letters. Read the story.

Mat sat.

Sam sat.

Mat sat. Sam sat.

Letter Cc

Cc

Say the picture name.
Listen to the beginning sound.
What sound do you hear?

The word **cat** begins with the
c sound, /k/.

Trace the letters.

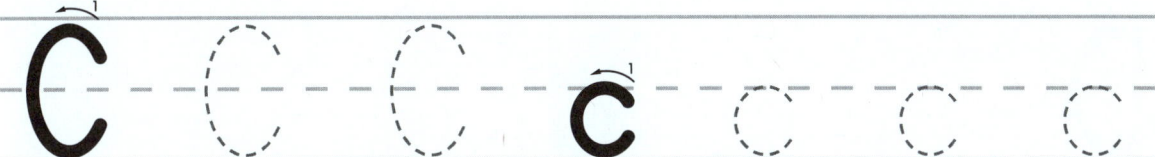

Say each picture name. If it begins with the c sound, /k/, circle the picture.

Letter Dd

Dd

Say the picture name.
Listen to the beginning sound.
What sound do you hear?

The word **dog** begins with the **d sound, /d/**.

Trace the letters.

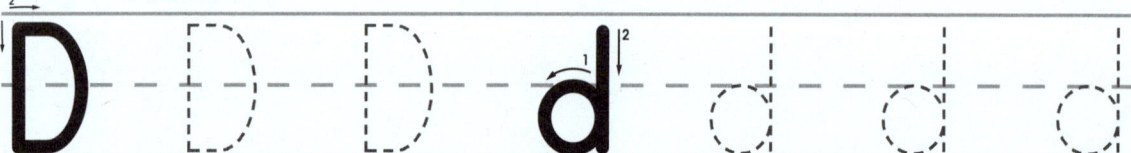

Say each picture name. If it begins with /d/, circle the picture.

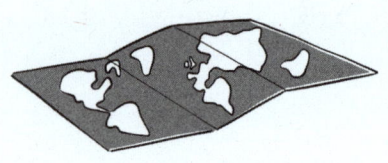

Read and Match

Say the name of each picture. Read each word. Draw a line from the picture to the word.

Read the sentence. If you hear /k/, circle the word.

A sad cat sat.

Rhyme Time!

Mat is making up a new jump rope rhyme! He needs words that rhyme with his name.

Read each word. Color the shapes with words that rhyme with *Mat*.

Mat

Story Time!

Trace the letters. Read the story.

The words *and* **and** *on* **can be sight words for now.**

Mat sat on Sam.

Sad Sam. Sad Mat. Sad cat.

Sam, cat, and Mat sat.

Letter Oo

Say the picture name.
Listen to the beginning sound.
What sound do you hear?

The word **octopus** begins with the **short o sound, /o/**.

Trace the letters.

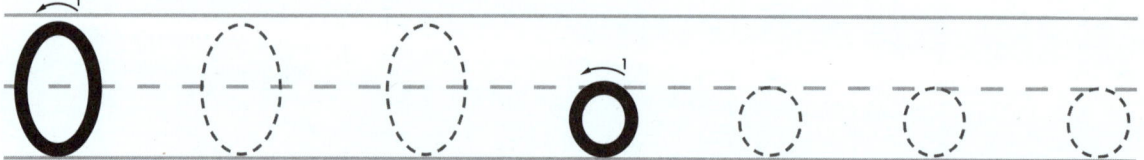

Color each uppercase O red.
Color each lowercase o blue.

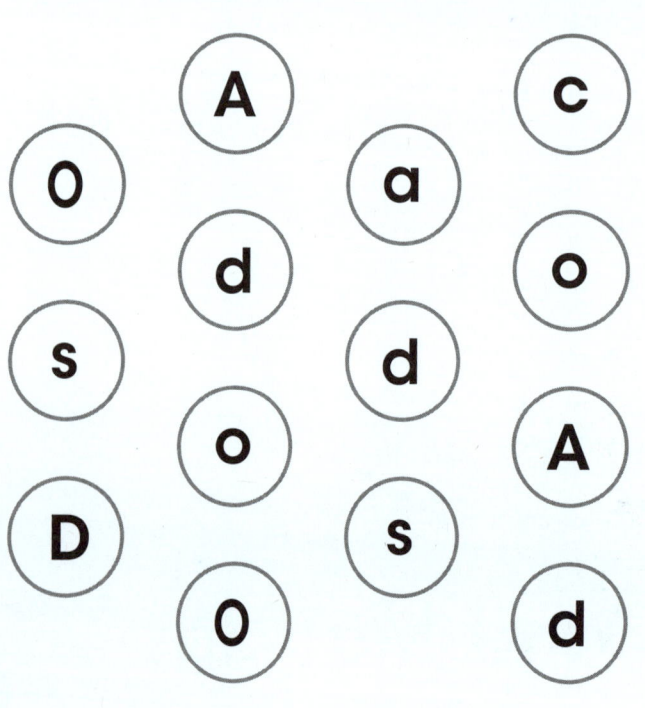

Say and Circle

Say each picture name. If it includes the short o sound, circle the picture.

Letter Hh

Say the picture name.
Listen to the beginning sound.
What sound do you hear?

The word **hat** begins with the
h sound, /h/.

Trace the letters.

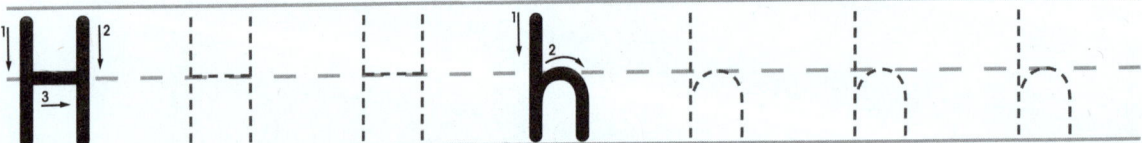

Say each picture name. If it begins with /h/, draw a line to *Hh*.

Letter Rr

Rr

Say the picture name.
Listen to the beginning sound.
What sound do you hear?

The word **rabbit** begins with the **r sound, /r/**.

Trace the letters.

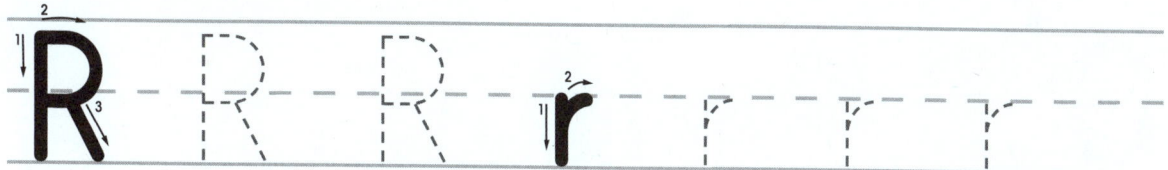

Say each picture name. If it begins with /r/, circle the picture.

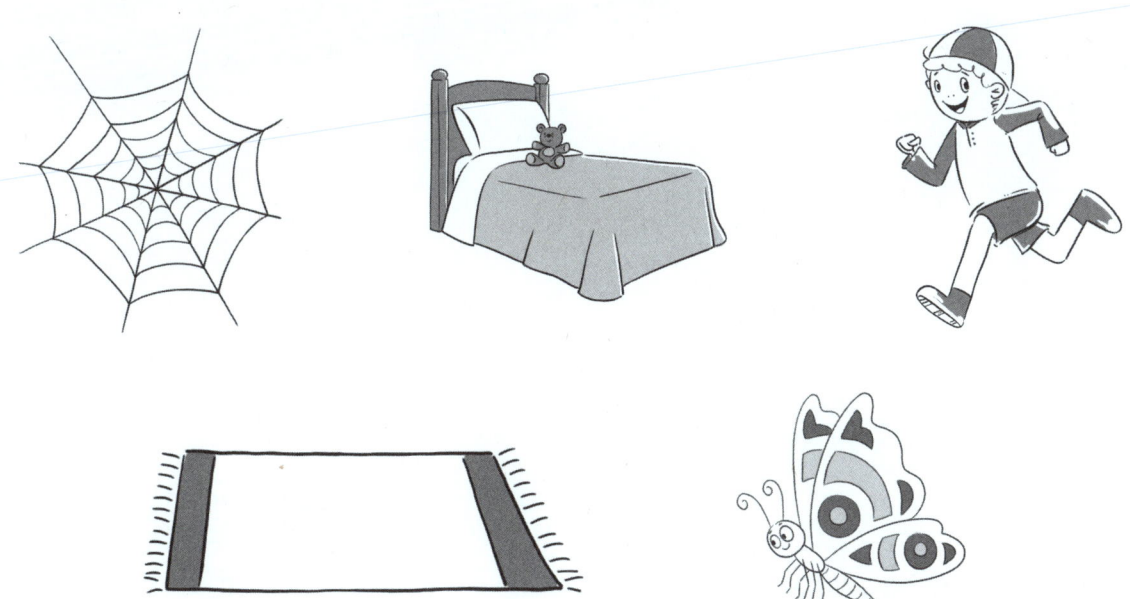

Letter Gg

Say the picture name.
Listen to the beginning sound.
What sound do you hear?

The word **goat** begins with the **g sound, /g/**.

Trace the letters.

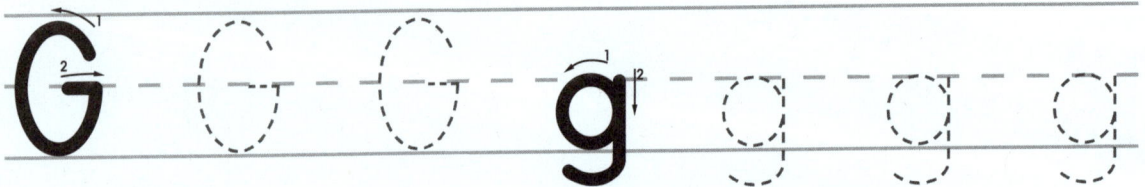

Say each picture name. If it begins with /g/, circle the picture.

 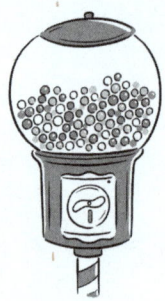 

What's the word?

This word starts with /g/. It's what some people wear on their faces to help them see better. What's the word?

Answer: glasses

Read and Match

Say each picture name. Read each word. Draw a line from the picture to the word.

   tag

   hog

   rag

Your Turn!

Draw a picture of a hog on a farm.

Rhyme Time!

Help Sam write a poem about his favorite dog, Mag!

Read each word. Circle the words that rhyme with *Mag*.

rag   rat

hat   sag

got   tag

Mag

Read and Match

Dot and Sam are looking for words that have the same vowel sounds as their names!

Read each word. Draw a line to connect words with the short *o* sound to Dot. Draw a line to connect words with the short *a* sound to Sam.

Story Time!

Trace the words. Read the story.

Dog **has a** hat.

Sad **dog.**

Dog **has a** rag hat!

Letter Bb

Bb

Say the picture name.
Listen to the beginning sound.
What sound do you hear?

The word **ball** begins with the
b sound, /b/.

Trace the letters.

Color each uppercase *B* red.
Color each lowercase *b* blue.

Say and Circle

Say each picture name. If it begins with /b/, circle the picture.

Say and Circle

Say each picture name. Circle the letter for the beginning sound.

t   s   b

d   h   c

g   r   s

b   m   d

What's the word?

This is what a ball does when it hits the ground. What's the word? What sound do you hear at the beginning?

Answer: bounce; /b/

Say and Match

Say each picture name. What is the middle sound? Draw a line to match the picture with the letter that stands for the middle sound.

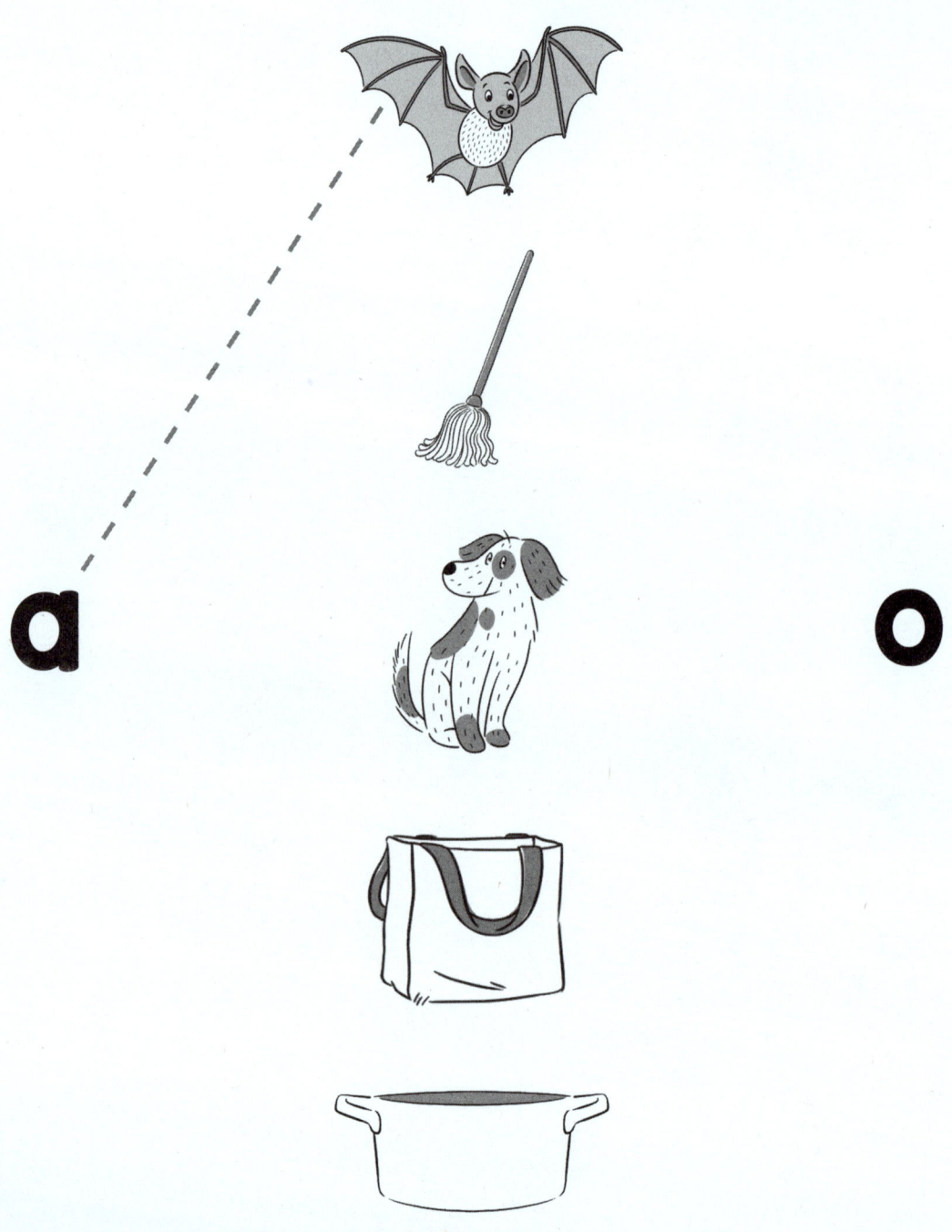

Tic-Tac-Toe

Say each picture name. Find three in a row that begin with /b/. Circle the pictures.

I spy!

Can you find three things around you that begin with /b/?

Trace and Read

Trace each letter to spell a word. Read the word.

bat

cab

bag

Read the sentence. If you hear /b/, circle the word.

Bat had a bag.

Rhyme Time!

Dot is dressed up as a bat!

Read each word. Color the leaves with words that rhyme with *bat*.

Word Maze

Mag got Sam's pad!

Start at Sam. Connect words with the short *a* sound to help Sam catch Mag.

Spell a Word

Say each picture name. Draw lines to connect letters and spell the word. Write the word on the line.

d — a — g
h — o — b   d o g

b — a — d
r — o — g

S — i — b
G — a — m

D — a — t
B — o — h

Story Time!

Trace the words. Read the story.

The cannot be sounded out; young readers must learn it as a sight word. **Can** is a sight word for now.

Mag had a rag.

Mac can tag Mag.

Mac got the rag.

Letter Ii

Say the picture name.
Listen to the beginning sound.
What sound do you hear?

The word **invitation** begins with the **short i sound, /i/**.

Trace the letters.

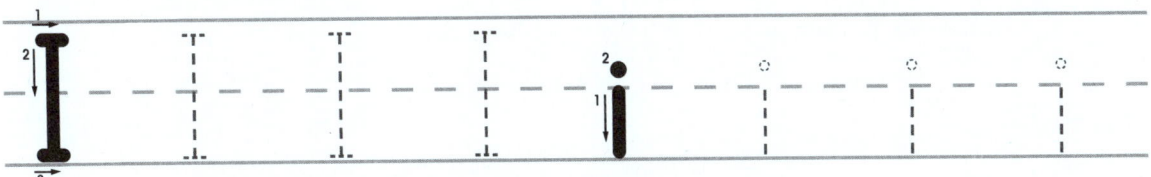

Say each picture name. If you hear the short *i* sound, color the picture.

Say and Circle

Say each picture name. If you hear the short *i* sound, circle the picture.

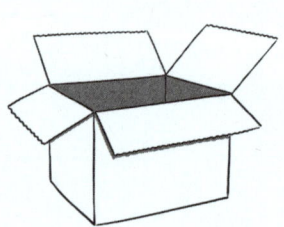 

Letter Nn

Say the picture name.
Listen to the beginning sound.
What sound do you hear?

The word **nest** begins with the n sound, /n/.

Trace the letters.

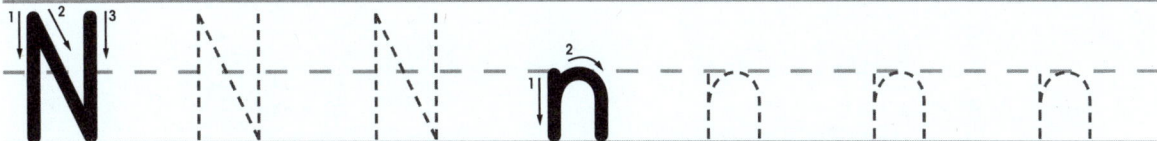

Say each picture name. If it begins with /n/, draw a line to *Nn*.

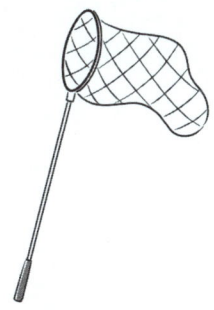

Nn

Say and Circle

Say each picture name. Circle the letter for the beginning sound.

i   g   h   b   r   n

n   r   g   o   n   d

What's the word?

You can smell thanks to this body part. What's the word? What sound do you hear at the beginning?

Answer: nose; /n/

Picture Maze

Nic and Mit are playing hide-and-seek.

Start at Nic. Connect pictures with the short *i* sound to help Nic find Mit the cat.

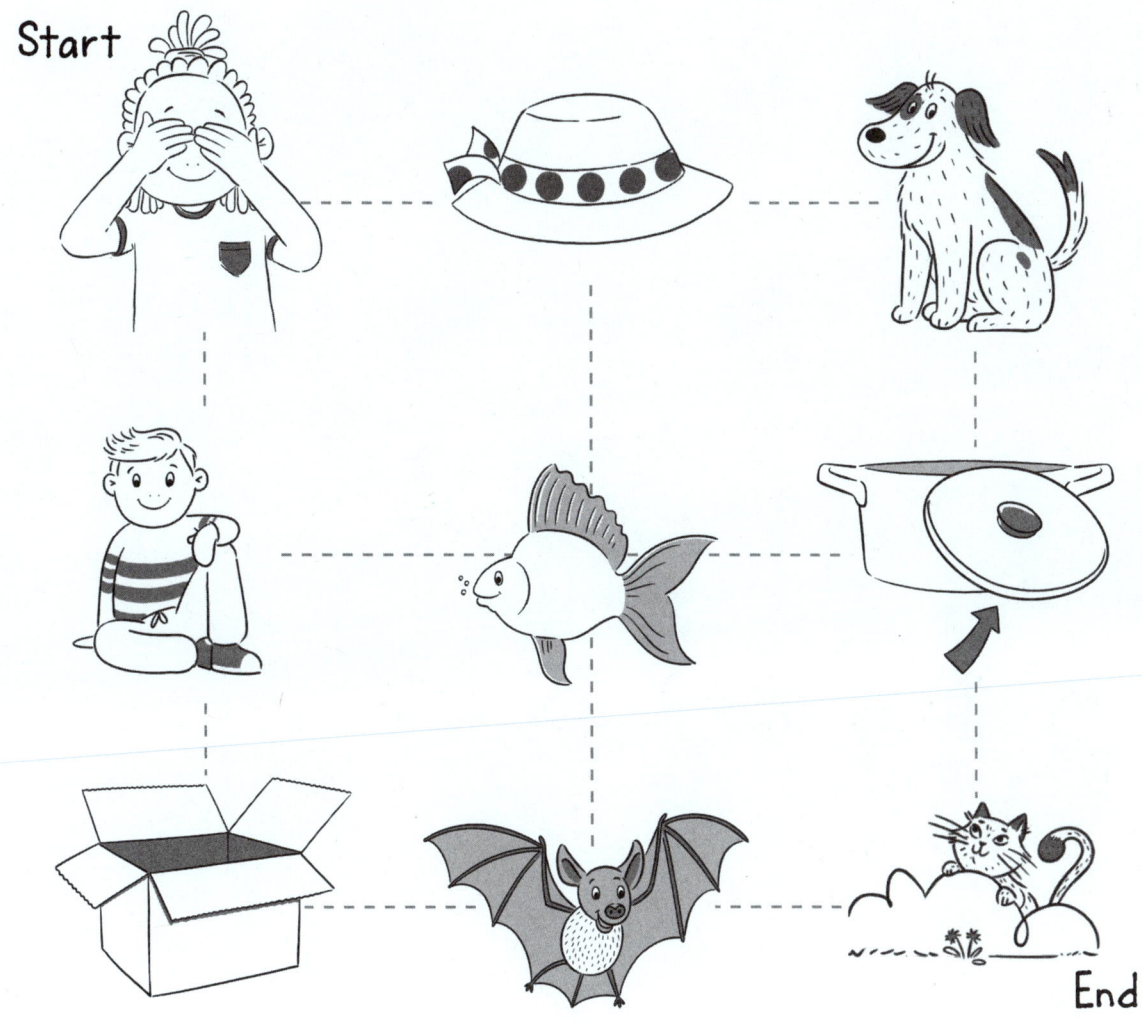

Spell a Word

Say each picture name. Draw lines to connect letters and spell the word. Write the word on the line.

Word Maze

Jig wants to play with Mit!

Start at Jig the pig. Connect words with the short *i* sound to help Jig find Mit the cat.

Trace and Circle

Trace each letter to spell a word. Read the word.

h d   b g

Say each picture name. If it begins with /n/, circle the picture.

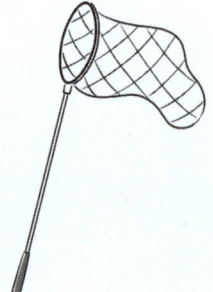   

Trace, Read, and Find

Trace each word, then read it. Find the picture that matches and circle it.

dig   hats

cab   dog

Story Time!

Trace the words. Read the story.

Dot hid.

Mat, Sam, and Dot hid.

Mit got Mat, Sam, and Dot.

Letter Pp

Say the picture name.
Listen to the beginning sound.
What sound do you hear?

The word **pig** begins with the
p sound, /p/.

Trace the letters.

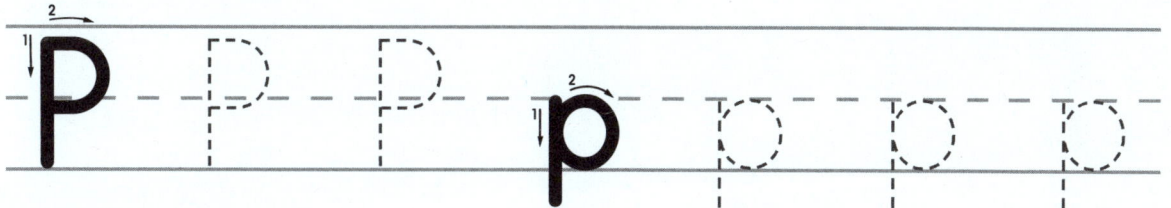

Say each picture name. Does it begin with /p/? Draw lines to connect pictures whose names begin with /p/.

  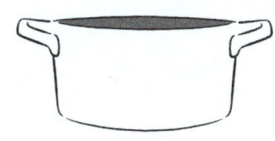

Letter Jj

Jj

Say the picture name.
Listen to the beginning sound.
What sound do you hear?

The word **jar** begins with the
j sound, /j/.

Trace the letters.

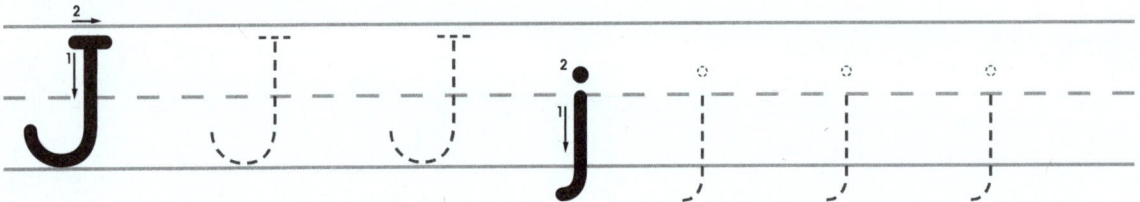

Say each picture name. If it begins with /j/, circle the picture.

Letter Ww

Say the picture name.
Listen to the beginning sound.
What sound do you hear?

The word **watch** begins with the
w sound, /w/.

Trace the letters.

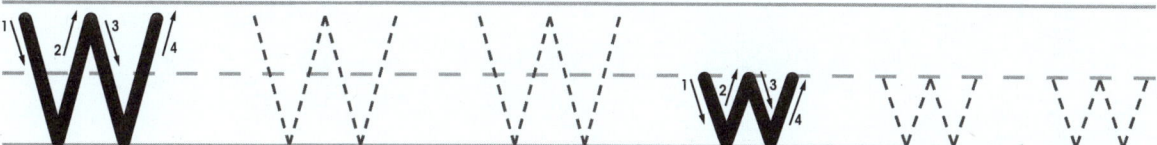

Say each picture name. If it begins with /w/, draw a line to *Ww*.

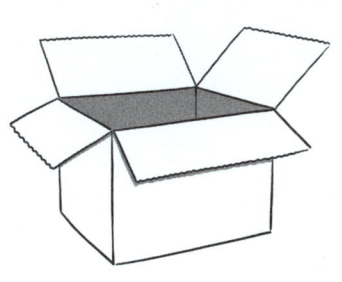

Ww

Say and Circle

Say each picture name. Circle the letter for the beginning sound.

j p w   j p w

j p w   j p w

What's the word?

This word is the name of a bird that is black-and-white and likes to swim. It begins with /p/. What's the word?

Answer: penguin

Say and Match

Say each picture name. What is the middle sound? Draw a line to match each picture with the letter that stands for the middle sound.

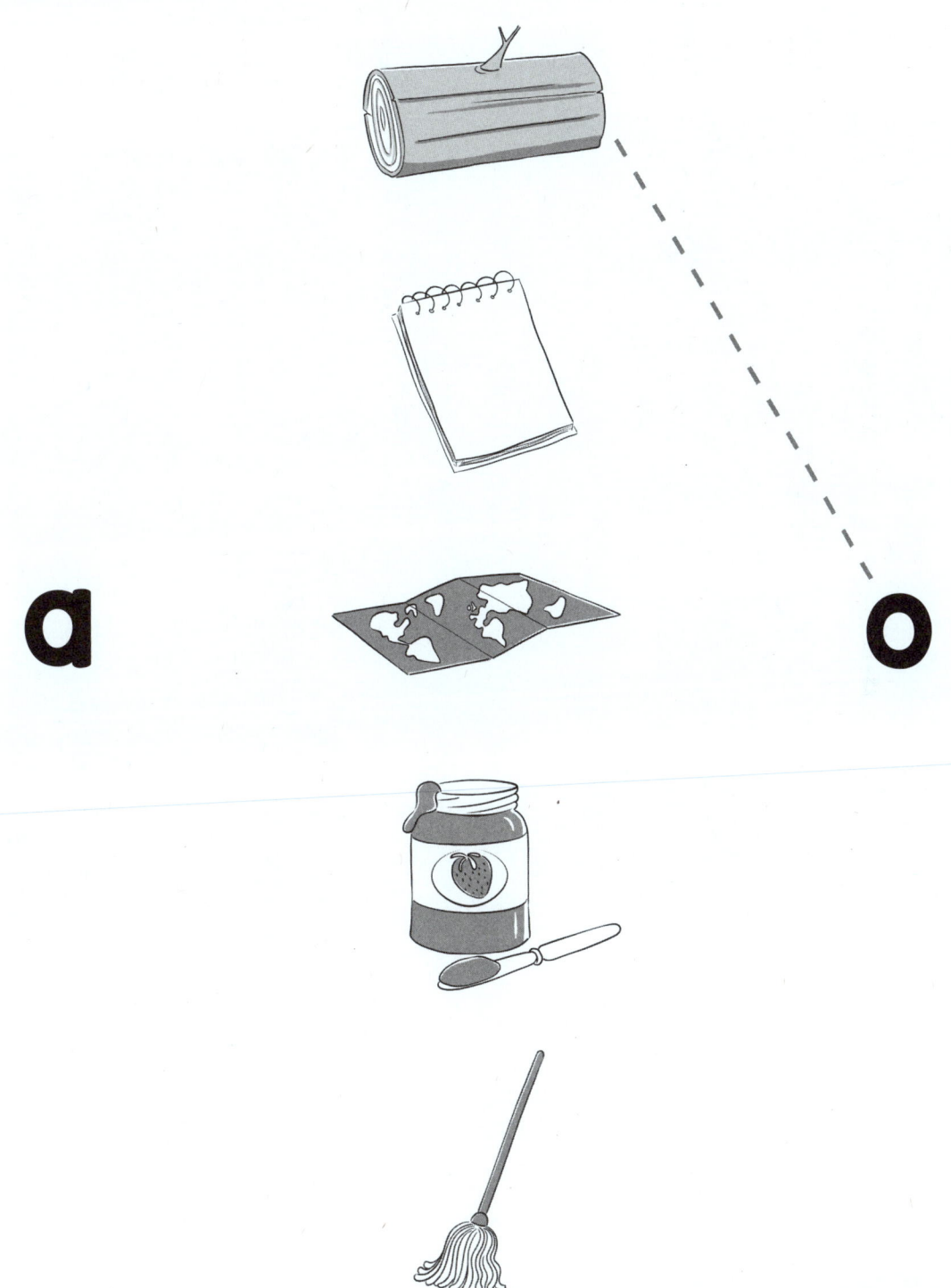

Trace, Read, and Find

Trace each word, then read it. Find the picture that matches and circle it.

pin   pop

wig   wag

Tic-Tac-Toe

Say each picture name. What sound do you hear at the <u>end</u> of the word? Find three in a row with the same ending sound. Circle the pictures.

I spy!

Can you find three things around you that end in the same sound?

Rhyme Time!

Nic is writing a new song for their band.

Read each word. On each list, circle the words that rhyme.

nap
map
jog

sip
win
pin

dog
tip
hog

Read and Draw

These animal friends are playing dress-up!

Fill in the missing letters to complete the words. Read the sentences.

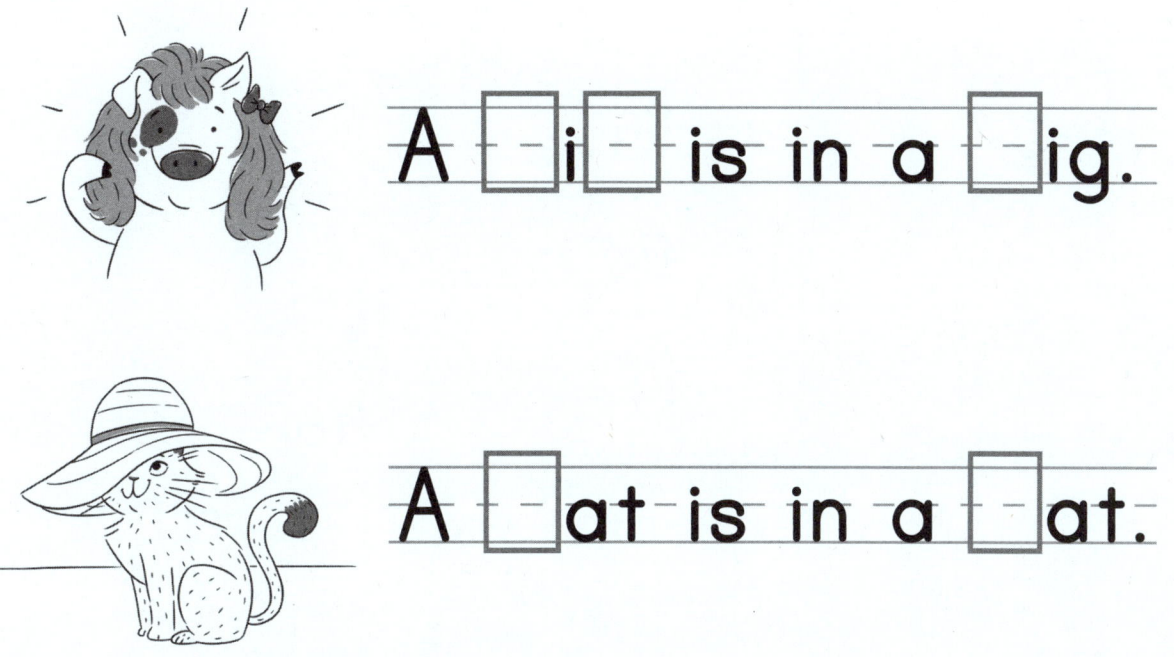

A ☐i☐ is in a ☐ig.

A ☐at is in a ☐at.

Your turn!

Draw yourself or a pet wearing a silly wig or hat!

Story Time!

Trace the words. Read the story.

Jig is a pig.

Jig can dig.

Jig can hop in.

Letter Uu

Say the picture name.
Listen to the beginning sound.
What sound do you hear?

The word **umbrella** begins with the **short u sound, /u/**.

Trace the letters.

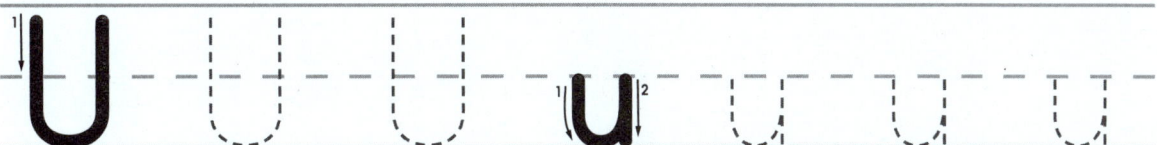

Say each picture name. If you hear the short *u* sound, circle the picture.

Letter Ff

Say the picture name.
Listen to the beginning sound.
What sound do you hear?

The word **feather** begins with the **f** sound, /f/.

Trace the letters.

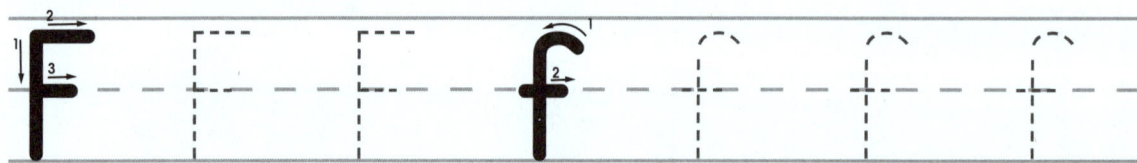

Fin and Fab need a hiding spot. Can they both fit?

Write F or f to complete each word. Read the sentences.

☐in can ☐it!

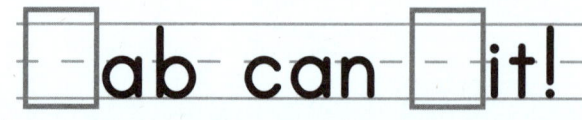
☐ab can ☐it!

Match and Draw

Say each picture name. If you hear the short *u* sound, draw a line to *Uu*.

 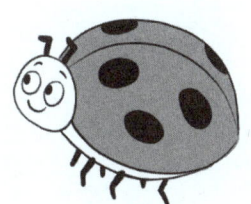

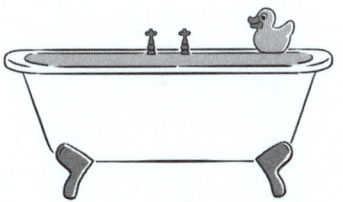 Uu

Your turn!

Draw a bug in a tub!

Say and Write

Say each picture name. Write the letter for the beginning sound.

Trace and Read

Trace each letter to complete the word. Read each word.

fun

win

fin

rug

Circle and Write

Mat and Sam found some fruit on the farm!

Read each word. Circle words that begin with /f/.

pig   jot

fog

nut

pop   kid   bin   jam

fan   pat   win   fun

Write the words that begin with /f/.

_____   _____   _____

Word Maze

Bud wants to hug his pet pug!

Start at Bud. Read each word. Connect words with the short *u* sound to help Bud hug his pug.

Read and Match

Read each word. Say each picture name. Draw a line from the word to the picture.

bus

van

net

fun

tug

Spell a Word

Say each picture name. Draw lines to connect letters and spell the word. Write the word on the line.

	n u s	
	b o g	bug

	g u p	
	f o m	___

	t u n	
	r i p	___

	h i g	
	m u w	___

63

Story Time!

Trace the words. Read the story.

Mac, Muff, and Ruff tug a rug.

Mac, Muff, and Ruff hid in it.

A rug is fun!

Letter Ee

Ee

Say the picture name. Listen to the beginning sound. What sound do you hear?

The word **elephant** begins with the **short e sound**, /e/.

Trace the letters.

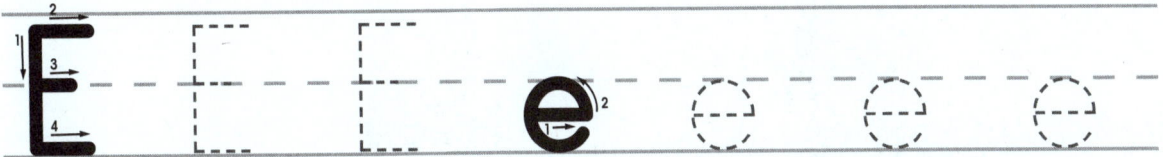

Say each picture name. If you hear the short e sound, circle the picture.

Say and Circle

Say each picture name. Circle the letter for the beginning sound.

h   c   t

w   n   r

h   m   g

s   f   b

What's the word?

This is a place where you might find animals and Old MacDonald. What's the word? What sound do you hear at the beginning?

Answer: farm; /f/

Letter Kk

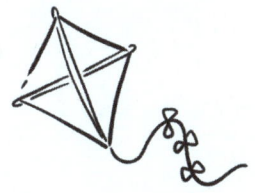

Say the picture name.
Listen to the beginning sound.
What sound do you hear?

The word **kite** begins with the
k sound, /k/.

Trace the letters.

Say each picture name. If it begins with /k/, draw a line to *Kk*.

Circle and Write

Kim is being kind to this kitten!

Read each word. Circle the words that begin with /k/.

wet   kit

nod   bat

tin   pep

net   kid   jug   bit

bun   Kim   pet   hen

Write the words that begin with /k/.

_____   _____   _____

68

Word Maze

Peg is running late. She needs to get on a jet!

Start at Peg. Read each word. Connect words with the short e sound to help Peg get to the jet on time.

Tic-Tac-Toe

Say each picture name. Find three in a row that begin with /k/. Circle the pictures.

What's the word?

This word is the name of something you might put on a hot dog or french fries. It begins with /k/. What's the word?

Answer: ketchup

Rhyme Time!

Ben loves his pet hen!

Read each word. Color the hearts with words that rhyme with *Ben* and *hen*.

Trace, Read, and Find

Trace and read each word. Say the name of each picture. If the word has the short *e* sound, circle the word and its picture.

net   bed

jam   web

Spell a Word

Say each picture name. Draw lines to connect letters and spell the word. Write the word on the line.

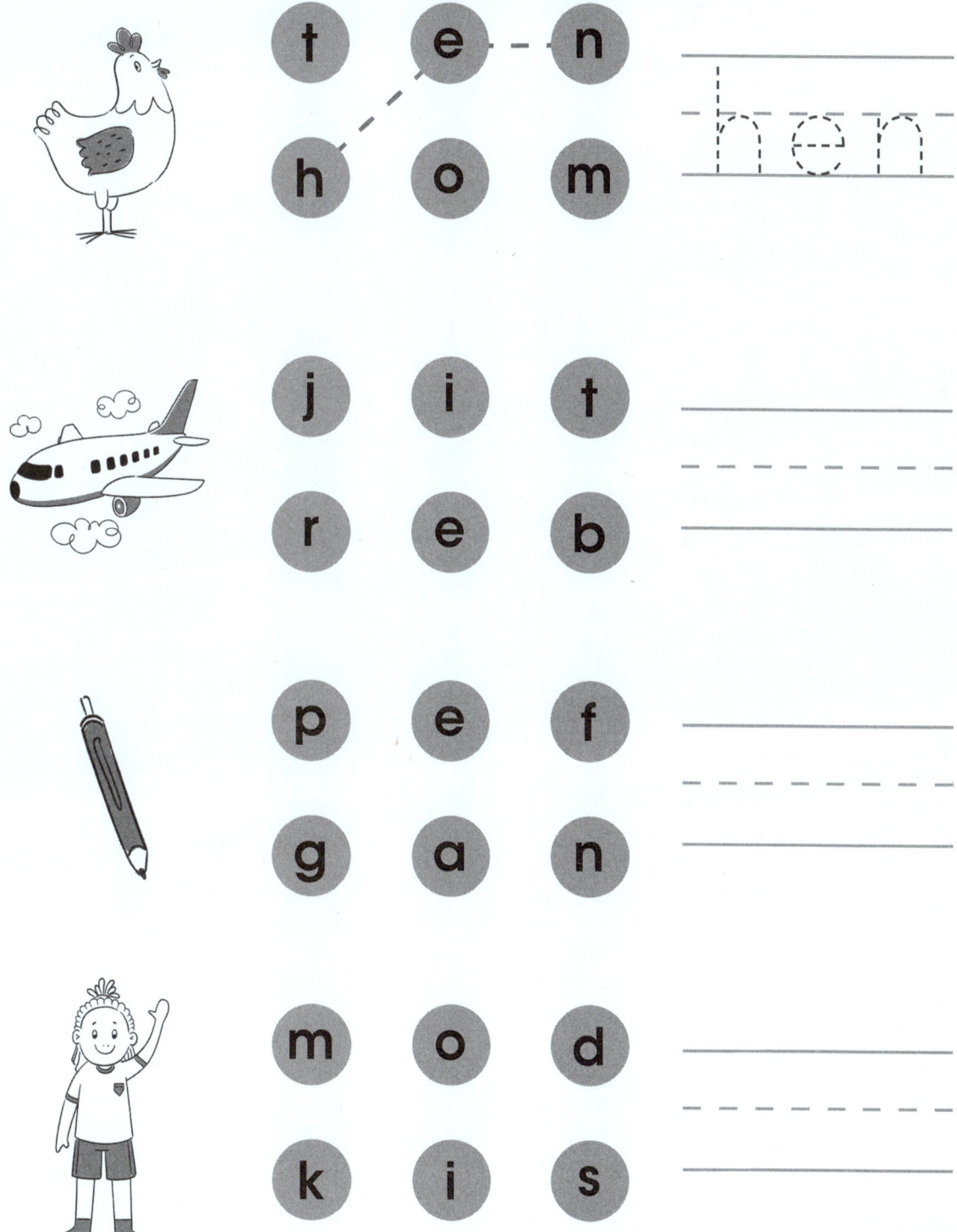

Story Time!

Trace the words. Read the story.

Ted had a red hen.

Red hen sits on a bed.

Red hen sits on a pig!

Letter Ll

Say the picture name.
Listen to the beginning sound.
What sound do you hear?

The word **lamp** begins with the l sound, /l/.

Trace the letters.

Say each picture name. If it begins with /l/, circle the picture.

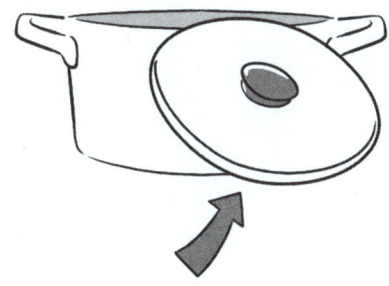

Letter Xx

Say the picture name.
Listen to the ending sound.
What sound do you hear?

The word **box** <u>ends</u> with the
x sound, /ks/.

Trace the letters.

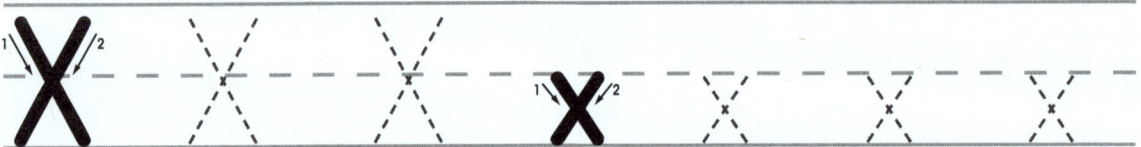

Color each uppercase *X* red.
Color each lowercase *x* blue.

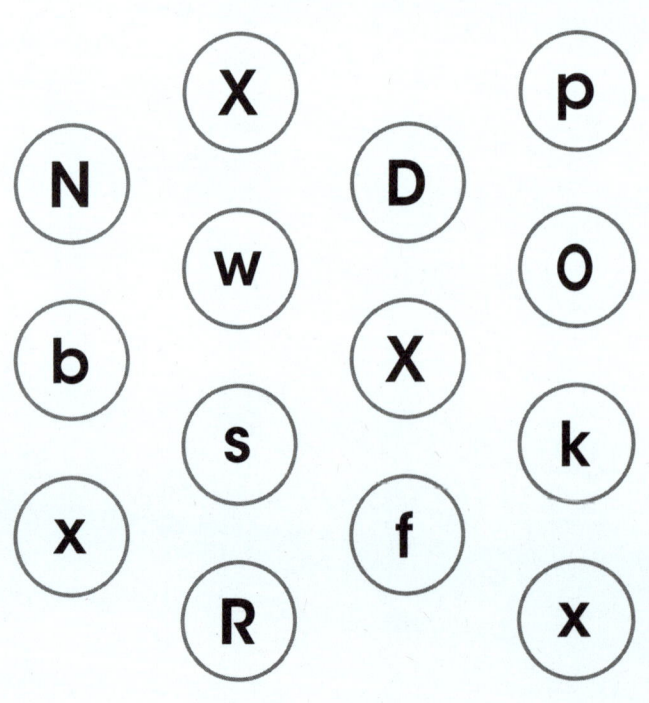

Read and Draw

These animal friends are being silly!

Fill in the missing letters to complete the words. Read the sentences.

Dog is on a ☐og.

Fo☐ is in a bo☐.

Your turn!

Draw a lion sitting on your lap!

77

Tic-Tac-Toe

Say each picture name. Find three in a row that end with the *x* sound, /ks/. Circle the pictures.

> **What's the word?**
>
> This is what you do with ingredients when you bake a cake. The word has the *x* sound, /ks/, at the end. What's the word?

Answer: mix

78

Word Maze

Liz spies a ladybug on the lawn!

Start at Liz. Connect words that begin with /l/ so Liz can say hi to the ladybug.

Spell a Word

Say each picture name. Draw lines to connect letters and spell the word. Write the word on the line.

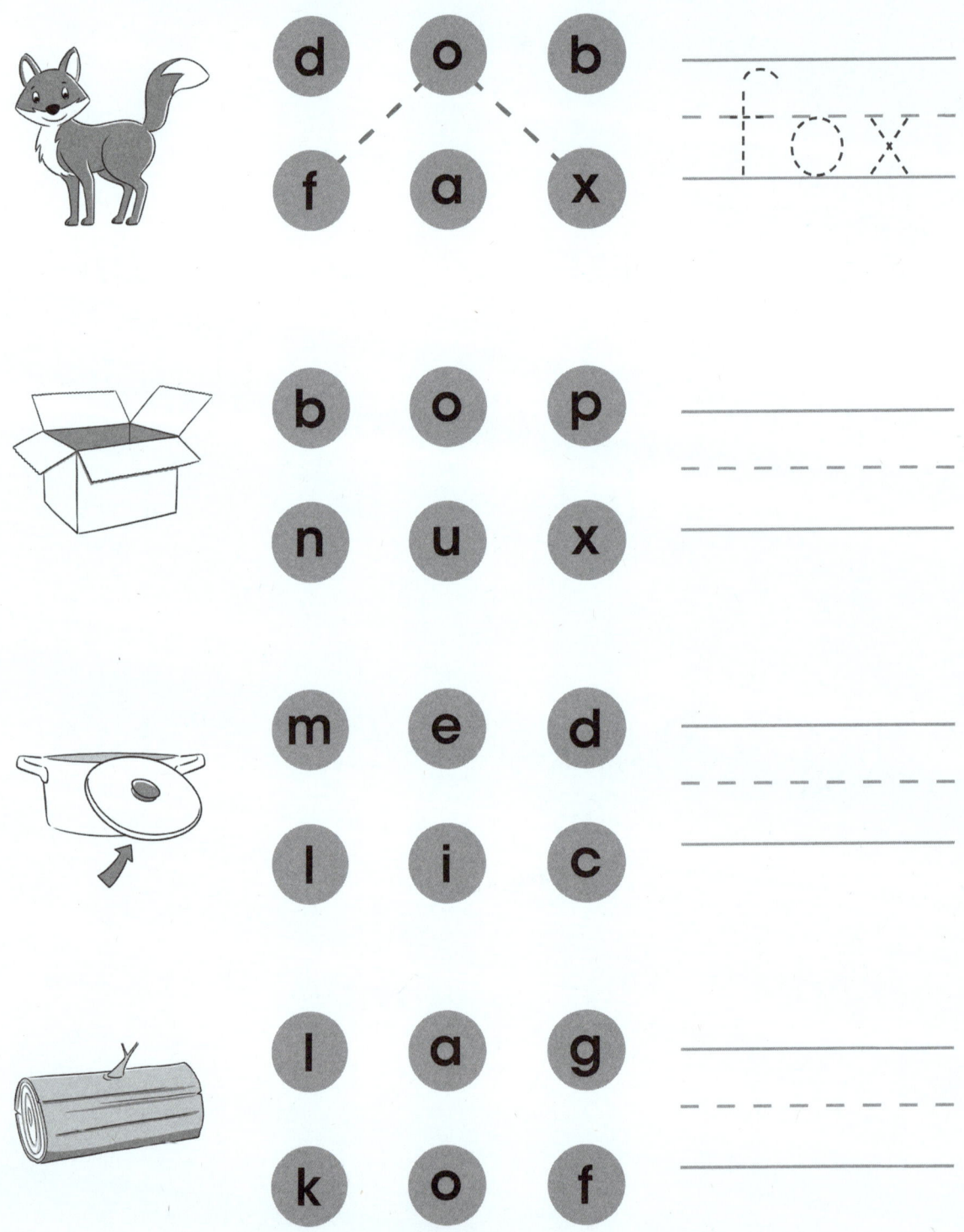

Say and Match

Say each picture name. What is the middle sound? Draw a line to match each picture with the letter that stands for the middle sound.

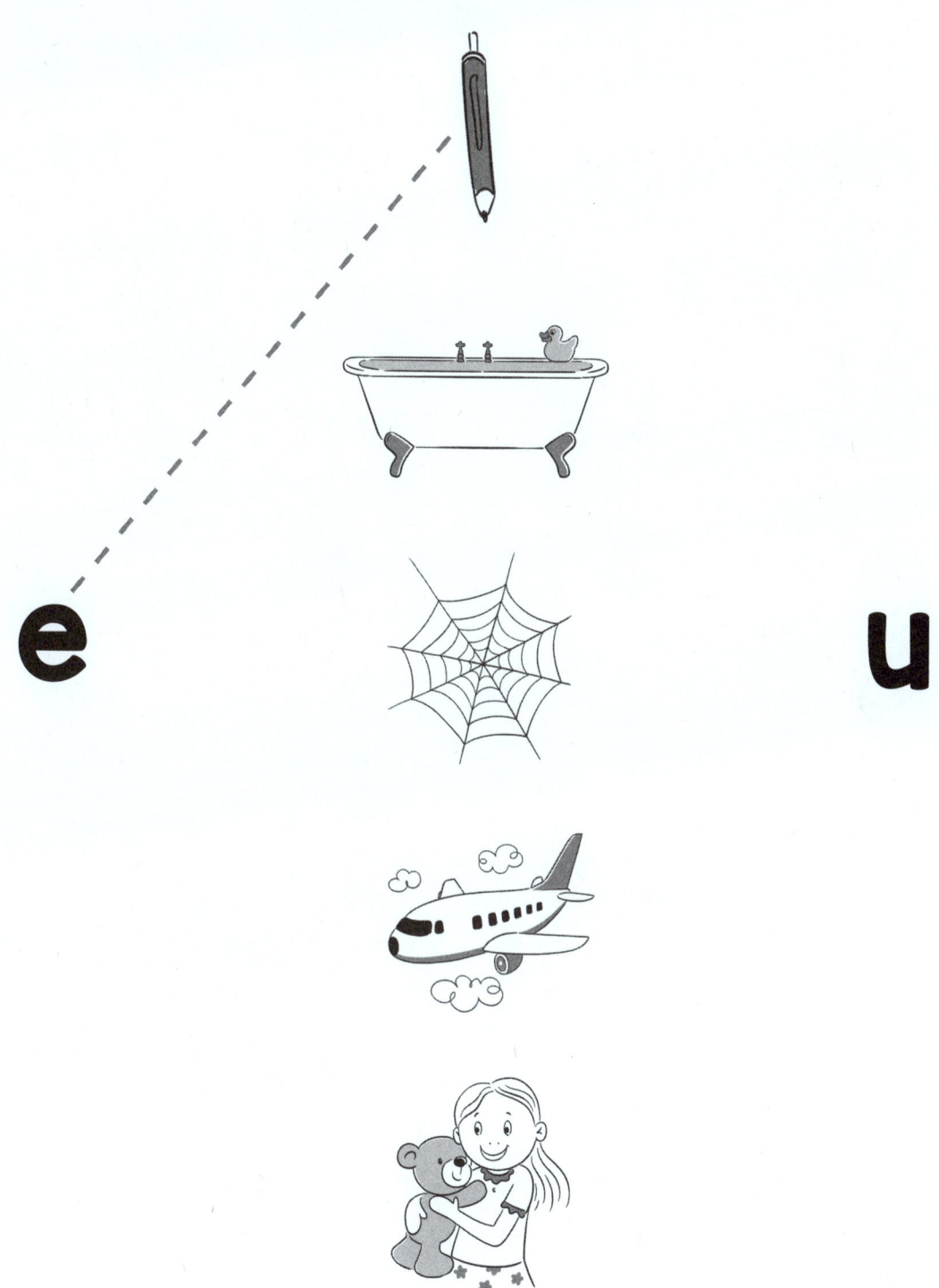

Rhyme Time!

Lad has six new kittens!

Read each word. Color the kittens with words that rhyme with *six*.

Story Time!

Trace the words. Read the story.

Lad had Kix the cat.

Kix had a box.

Kix had six kits in the box!

Letter Vv

Say the picture name.
Listen to the beginning sound.
What sound do you hear?

The word **valentine** begins with the v sound, /v/.

Trace the letters.

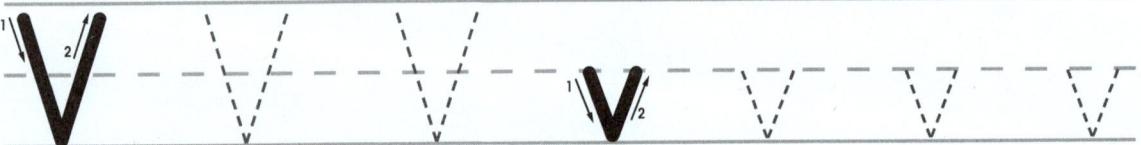

Say each picture name. If it begins with /v/, circle the picture.

Letter Yy

Say the picture name.
Listen to the beginning sound.
What sound do you hear?

The word **yo-yo** begins with the
y sound, /y/.

Trace the letters.

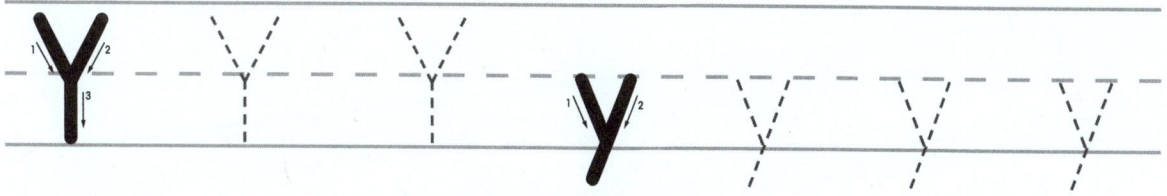

Read the sentence. Circle the word that begins with /y/.

Yes! Jin is in a big hat.

Letter Zz

Zz

Say the picture name.
Listen to the beginning sound.
What sound do you hear?

The word **zebra** begins with the z sound, /z/.

Trace the letters.

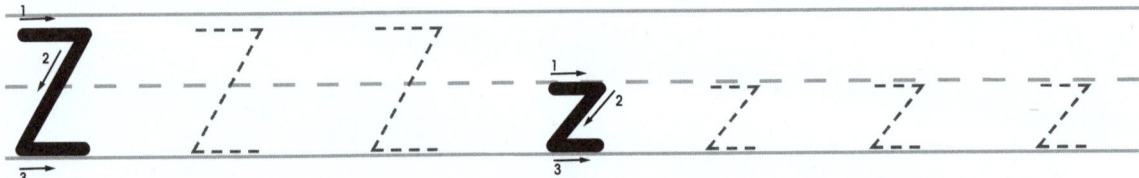

Color each uppercase Z red.
Color each lowercase z blue.

Read and Match

Read each word. Say each picture name. Draw a line from the word to the picture.

zip

van

yum

Your turn!

Draw a picture of something you like to eat. Yum!

Word Maze

Jaz drew a picture for Liz!

Start at Jaz. Connect words that *begin or end* with /z/ to help Jaz deliver her picture to Liz.

Letter Qq

Say the picture name.
Listen to the beginning sound.
What sound do you hear?

The word **queen** begins with the **qu sound, /kw/**.

Q is always followed by u. Together, these letters stand for the sound /kw/.

Trace the letters.

Say each picture name. If it begins with the *qu* sound, /kw/, circle the picture.

Read and Match

Say the name of each picture. Read each word. Draw a line from the picture to the word.

quick

quack

quilt

What's the word?

This is another word for "test." It begins with the *qu* sound, /kw/. What's the word?

Trace and Read

Trace each letter to complete the word. Read the word.

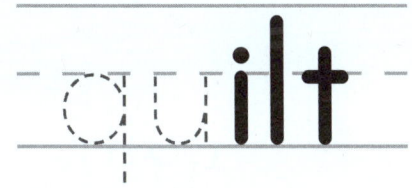 

Circle and Write

Vroom! Here comes the vet in her van!

Read each word. Circle words that begin with /v/.

quilt   cup

tag

vest

fin   red   kit   lid

van   bun   quack   vet

Write the words that begin with /v/.

_____   _____   _____

Story Time! (Part 1)

Fill in the missing letters. Read the story.

To cannot be sounded out; young readers must learn it as a sight word.

A ⬚et had a ⬚an.

A ca⬚ had a cut leg.

The v⬚t had to fix the c⬚t.

Story Time! (Part 2)

Fill in the missing letters. Read the story.

The cat ran zig☐ag.

The vet g☐t the cat. Zam!

The ☐at and the ☐et sat.

"I read the whole book!"®

Name: _____

worked hard and finished the

Beginning Phonics
WORKBOOK

BOB BOOKS